NAISOLA'S SUPER FUTURE

By Deborah Nabubwaya Chambers, MPH, MHA

Illustrated by Katie African, Sanaa Naisola Naimasiah,
Caedmon Lemayian Chambers,
Enzo Xolani Chambers, and Alaia Shwari Chambers

This book is dedicated to my children Caedmon Lemayian Chambers, Enzo Xolani Chambers, and Alaia Shwari Chambers. All brown and black children are loved and celebrated. You can overcome any setbacks that come your way. Embrace life and be confident as you face new experiences and life changes. Release all your negative thoughts and replace them with positive ones that bring joy to your life and others around you. Nawapenda sana!

\- D. N. C

Published in the United States by Deborah Nabubwaya Chambers

ISBN: 9798421407331

MAP OF AFRICA

Naisola, a gorgeous eight-year-old girl who lives in a small city in Kenya, has big dreams and likes to draw superheroes. She believes superheroes are the good guys who help other children when they have unwanted feelings.

Naisola likes to play a good soccer game with her six close friends.

When bored, they imagined themselves as superheroes playing soccer with their fantastic costumes and terrific magnets, which made the ball flow as fast or slow as they wanted. The main rule for this game included not stepping on the ball to stop it from moving.

One sunny Saturday morning, Naisola and her friends went to the neighborhood playground to play a soccer game. Unfortunately, two of her friends tried to change the rules by stepping on the ball while moving.

This change of rules eventually made them annoyed at each other. Naisola and her friends decided to stop playing soccer for the day because not everyone followed the main rule. These bad feelings made everyone uncomfortable and sad.
Stop the game!

Naisola had the superpower of finding answers to most of her problems. She did her best not to stay in a bad mood for a very long time. Naisola had learned some precious lessons from her cousins Likizo and Eshaka when they visited her family from the United States.
I do my best to make good choices to forgive my friends if they hurt me or say something bad about me. If I did something wrong to my friends, I ask them to forgive me.
Naisola, whenever you are angry or sad during playtime, please sit down with your friends and face those bad feelings. Choose to find a good feeling that will chase the bad feelings away.

Naisola thought about her friends on the first day of school when they were all nervous and did not know what to expect. They all felt lonely and frightened after their parents had dropped them off early in the morning at the playground, just before the first class of the year started.

Luckily, they were assigned to Mrs. Uwezo's class. She was a kind, caring, and excellent teacher who had superpowers of years of experience teaching children.

Naisola remembered what Mrs. Uwezo told her during the first week of school.

If you ever feel frightened about making new friends at the playground, take some steps forward and say hello to a new friend. Share your name and invite your friend to play with you.

Naisola eventually mastered her superpower of confidence and boldly got up to talk to her friends. Suddenly, she remembered how happy she was to have good friends who enjoyed playing outside with her in school and the neighborhood playground.
Marafiki, let us be kind to each other and enjoy playing soccer. We are friends, and we have the superpowers of kindness and forgiveness.

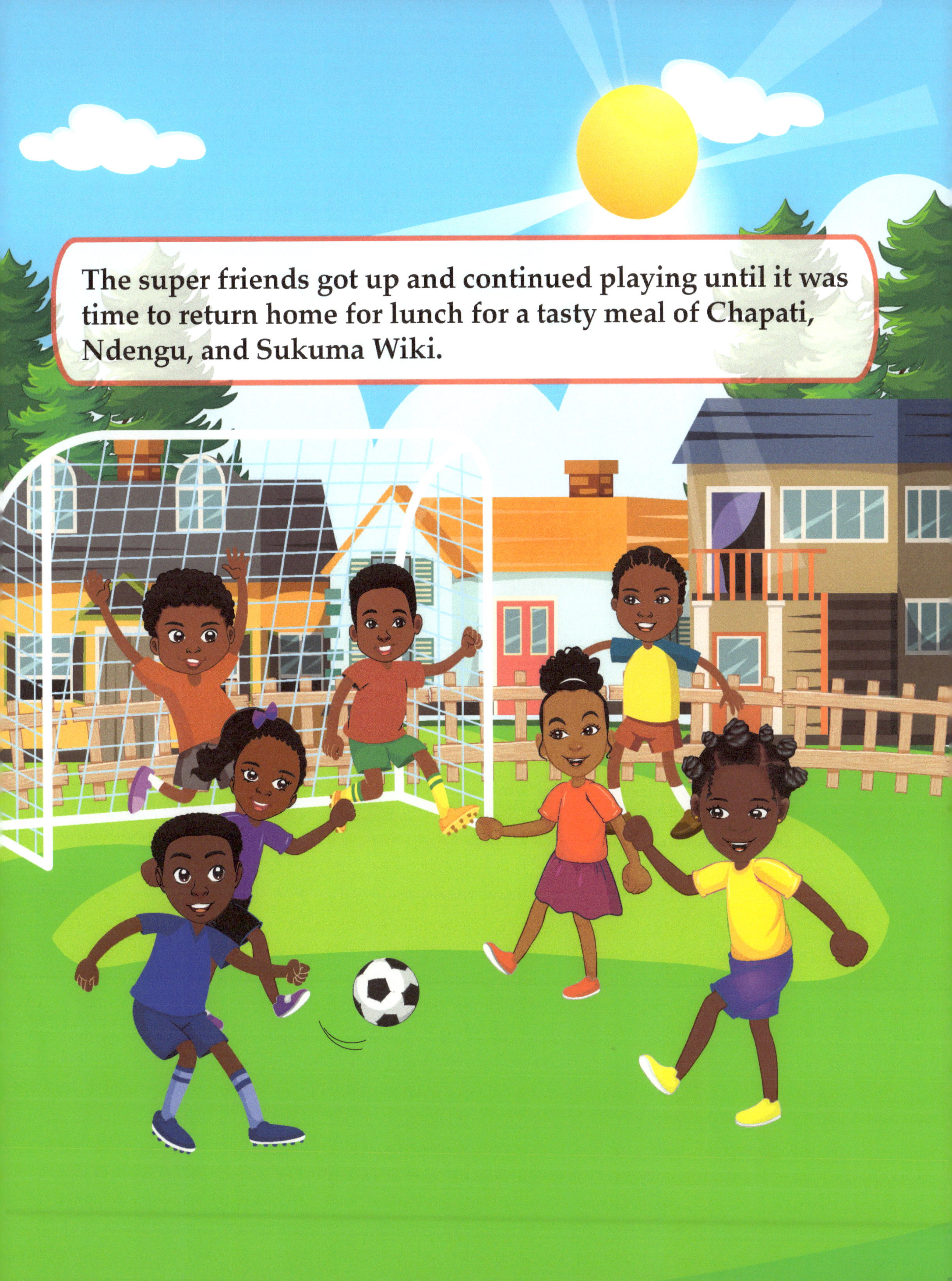
The super friends got up and continued playing until it was time to return home for lunch for a tasty meal of Chapati, Ndengu, and Sukuma Wiki.

During dinner, Naisola told her family how she and her friends were thrilled to find an answer that replaced their fear and helped them play peacefully. Naisola and her friends learned to face their sad, worried, angry, uncomfortable, nervous, lonely, frightened, and bored feelings. Choosing to solve their problems encouraged them to be peaceful, motivated, confident, excited, creative, happy, and kind.

MAP OF AFRICA

shwari

LEARN SWAHILI WITH NAISOLA AND HER SUPER FRIENDS

Marafiki means friends
Chapati means flatbread
Ndengu means lentils
Sukuma Wiki means Kale or Collard Greens mixed with onions and tomatoes

CHAPATI RECIPE
By Deborah Nabubwaya Chambers

Ingredients

4 ¾ cups of whole wheat flour
1 teaspoon of salt
2 cups of warm water
1 cup of cooking oil. Adjust amount as needed.

Directions

1. Mix the ingredients together.
   Oil contributes to making the chapati soft so add a bit of it at this step to your recipe.
2. Knead your flour on a clean surface for 5 minutes.
3. Cover it with a cling film at room temperature for 15 minutes or a few hours to give it time to rest before rolling into even sized balls of dough.

4. Sprinkle a small amount of flour on your surface to prevent the dough from sticking on the surface then place one ball of dough.
5. Roll the ball of dough with a rolling pin.
6. Spread a thin layer of oil on your circular chapati. This helps to make the chapatis soft.
7. Roll the circular chapati into a cone then press the cone into a ball. This step is what produces layers in the chapati.
8. Repeat the above step for all the balls of dough.
9. Roll the first ball into a circular chapati. Pre-heat your cooking pan and keep the heat to medium heat to avoid burning the chapatis.
10. Do not start with oil in the pan. Cook it dry for the first side for about a minute then turn to cook the other side. Add a small amount of oil and cook until the chapati browns a bit. Regulate the heat to medium heat and reduce the heat if they cook fast.
11. Turn the chapati and cook the other side. When both sides are brown and cooked, place on a plate. Your chapati is ready.

SUKUMA WIKI RECIPE

Ingredients

Two bunches of Kale/Collard Greens
1 red onion
2 tomatoes
A pinch of salt
Cooking oil

Directions

1. Thoroughly wash your Kale or Collard Greens.
2. Cut them into small sizes.
3. Cut your red onion into small pieces.
4. Cut your tomatoes into small cubes.
5. Add ¼ cup of oil to a preheated pot.
6. Add the red onions then mix for a minute.
7. Add the tomatoes then mix for another minute
8. Add a pinch of salt. Mix your ingredients well.
9. Add your Sukuma wiki in small portions and stir to ensure all the ingredients mix well. Cook for 4 minutes then serve.

NDENGU (LENTILS) RECIPE

Prepare your ndengu (lentils) according to your favorite lentil stew recipe. You can add a cup of coconut milk for an extra creamy and tasty flavor.

SPECIAL THANKS!

A special thank you to my family that continues to create unparalleled spaces for my dreams to bloom into reality. A hearty thank you to our Ohio family, Florent Msoshi Benga, Eunice Mwamini Benga, and their boys. Your incredible contributions, patience, skills, knowledge, friendship, and encouragement light my path. You are so valued and are important. Thank you to Megan Kusch and her family for your friendship, talents, support, and everything else in between. You are so treasured and are precious! May God bless you.

Bringing published writers into classrooms, public libraries, bookstores, home libraries and promoting virtual author visits are all effective ways of inspiring our children to develop a passion for reading and writing from a very early age. I remain grateful to Mrs. Lauren Heffelfinger and Mrs. Jamie Taylor. They shine at igniting a spark of innovation, motivating our children, drawing out their sense of self-confidence, and boosting their discovery of talents. These ladies excel at enhancing literacy by their unparalleled contributions in their classrooms.

Naisola's Super Future is about creativity, representation, friendship, promoting physical activity outdoors, and problem-solving. Children will discover their superpowers of finding solutions to their problems, replacing negative thoughts with positive thoughts that encourage peace and joy to all, and appreciating other cultures.

ABOUT THE AUTHOR

Deborah Nabubwaya Chambers, MPH, MHA, is a vibrant public health and healthcare administration professional that has always enjoyed reading and writing. Her work has been published in peer-reviewed journal articles and book chapters. She enjoys writing children's books during her free time. Every interaction with students inspires her to read and write with renewed energy and purpose. She highly promotes literacy at any opportunity because she believes education will take us to places we have never stepped before. Our children will explore worlds both near and far. It will open doors for others to realize their dreams.

Deborah is beyond thankful for spaces created in our communities and globally so that our children know from an early age that they are loved, they are so important, and they discover the value to learn, embrace, and appreciate diverse cultures. Her writing is one of the ways she fosters healthy communities. She lives and works in Ohio, where she is determined to explore as many hiking trails with her family as possible.